MODERN
F·A·B·L·E·S

S. MICHAEL WILCOX & TED L. GIBBONS
ILLUSTRATED BY MARK MCCUNE

ISBN 13: 978-1-59955-307-8

Published by CFI, an imprint of Cedar Fort, Inc.
2373 W. 700 S., Springville, UT 84663
Distributed by Cedar Fort, Inc., www.cedarfort.com

LIBRARY OF CONGRESS CATALOGING-IN-PUBLICATION DATA

Gibbons, Ted.
  Modern fables / Ted L. Gibbons, S. Michael Wilcox ; illustrated by Mark McCune.
     p. cm.
  ISBN 978-1-59955-307-8 (acid-free paper)
  1. Fables, American. 2. Animals--Juvenile fiction.
  [1. Fables. 2. Animals--Fiction.] I. Wilcox, S. Michael. II. McCune, Mark, ill. III. Title.

  PZ8.2.G45Mod 2010
  [Fic]--dc22

                         2010004646

Cover and book design by Angela D. Olsen
Edited by Heidi Doxey
Cover design © 2011 by Lyle Mortimer

Printed on acid-free paper

Printed in China

10 9 8 7 6 5 4 3 2 1

MODERN
F·A·B·L·E·S

S. MICHAEL WILCOX & TED L. GIBBONS
ILLUSTRATED BY MARK McCUNE

BONNEVILLE BOOKS
SPRINGVILLE, UTAH

DEDICATION

TO ALL THOSE WHO READ TO US
WHEN WE WERE CHILDREN,
AND ALL THOSE WHO
READ TO CHILDREN TODAY.

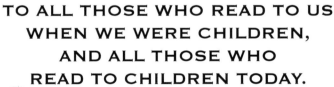

CONTENTS

ONCE THERE WAS A SNAKE NAMED Sidney who cried every day: *"I am the most unfortunate animal in the desert."*

"Why are you so unhappy?" his friends asked him.

"Because I want to wear trousers," he said. *"All of you can wear trousers. Even my first cousin, Larry the Lizard, can wear shorts. I can't think of any creature in the whole desert that can't wear pants of some kind."*

He was very sad and never wanted to go anywhere, so he stayed coiled under his rock day after day and sulked.

"Half a pair of pants is better than no pants at all," his friends told him. *"You can fit in one leg. Try these on."*

"But what do I do with the other leg?" They tried various devices. They tried wrapping the extra leg around and around his body. But then he couldn't crawl. They tried tying it in knots to shorten it,

but the knots kept getting caught in the crooks of tree limbs and under rocks.

They tried just letting it drag, but soon it was filled with burrs and cactus spines. They tried cutting the extra pant leg off. But all the seams came unraveled.

"It's no use," Sidney sighed as he slithered back under his rock to brood. One by one his friends crept away and left him alone.

And there he would have stayed had Sabrina not crawled by. *"Why are you so unhappy?"* she asked him.

"Go away!" he said grumpily.

"Maybe I can help," Sabrina offered.

"I'm sad because all of my friends can wear trousers except me."

"I know just what you mean," Sabrina said. *"I've always wanted to wear pants too, but I never know what to do with the other leg."*

"Saaay," Sidney said smiling. *"Do you think . . . ?"*

IF YOU CAN'T DO IT ALONE, FIND A FRIEND!

"Maybe . . ."

"Perhaps . . ."

"We'll never know unless we try." So Sidney and Sabrina both crawled into one leg of the pants and slithered off together, which was the beginning of a long and lasting friendship.

ONE MORNING FERDINAND THE Ferret woke up feeling very hungry. *"What a fine day for hunting,"* he said. *"I shall have a moose steak for breakfast."* And he set off whistling with high hopes.

He soon found a moose and leaped onto his back, but the moose threw Ferdinand off into the mud. And the ferret was hungrier still.

"Well," he said, undaunted. *"For brunch I will settle for one of the great bucks of the forest."*

Off he set again, humming softly to himself.

At ten o'clock he leaped on a great buck, but the buck shook his antlers and flung Ferdinand into the branches. And the ferret was hungrier still.

"Well," he said, *"A fat feathered turkey for lunch will taste just fine."* Singing to himself, he plunged into the forest once again.

At noon he found a fat feathered turkey, but the turkey beat Ferdinand soundly about the head and shoulders with his wings. And the ferret was hungrier still.

"Perhaps my luck would change if, for a mid-afternoon snack, I hunted a red squirrel."

Into the forest he skipped once again, and at three o'clock he spied a red squirrel high in a tree. He began to climb, but the squirrel bombarded Ferdinand with nuts and branches. And the ferret was hungrier still.

At six o'clock, as the sun was setting, he caught a shrew.

"A shrew will do," Ferdinand said, as he went home whistling. And he had a very fine supper.

ONCE UPON A TIME 1001 PIGS were placed together in a great fenced field.

When it was time to eat their first meal together, the pigs ambled over to the pig troughs to have their swill. Some of them had terrible manners.

"*Me first!*" cried one.

"*Out of my way!*" cried another.

"*Take that!*" yelled a third as he pushed his neighbor right into the trough.

But his neighbor liked it there because he got more of the food. Soon all of them were in the troughs. All of them except one, a pig named Hamlet who watched as they ate and splashed and slobbered in their food till it was all over them.

"*I just can't live like that,*" Hamlet said.

He put on his tie and his dinner jacket and then searched along the fence line and at the bottom of the field until he found some acorns and watercress and wild raspberries. Then he set his table with a linen cloth, his best china, and a candle and had a quiet, clean meal, all alone.

"*The swill is swell if you don't mind the smell!*" his comrades cried to him. But he paid no attention.

After dinner, they were filthy. *"Let's go to the pond and bathe,"* said one.

They rushed to the pond. But some of them had terrible manners.

"Me first!" cried one.

"Out of my way!" cried another.

"Take that!" yelled a third as he pushed his neighbor right into the mud at the edge of the pond. But he liked it there because the mud was cool and covered the food on his back and legs. Soon all of the pigs were wallowing in the mud.

All of them except Hamlet, who watched as they rolled and wallowed in the mud till it was all over them.

"I just can't live like that," he said.

He took his towel and soap and walked to the other side of the pond, where he washed his hooves and snout and combed his bristles.

"It's great to wallow! Just remember not to swallow!" his comrades cried to him. But he paid no attention.

This went on for many weeks and 1000 pigs got fatter and filthier while Hamlet stayed clean and lean.

One day a large truck backed up to the gate. The pigs were herded one by one into the truck.

The driver silently watched the pig procession until Hamlet came by.

"Wait!" he cried. *"Something must be wrong with this pig. He is neither fat nor filthy! Leave him here."*

So Hamlet returned to his dinner, and the truck took 1000 pigs to the sausage factory.

> 1000 FAT AND FILTHY PIGS CAN BE WRONG!

"EVERYTHING IS WHITE!" Porter the Polar Bear cried. *"The snow is white. The ice is white. I am white. When the wind blows, even the water is white. I want some color in my life! I'm tired of the North Pole."*

Porter knew that Carl the Caribou ran a travel agency. He spent an afternoon looking at brochures.

"I am going south to Hawaii," he finally announced. *"There I will see many beautiful colors."*

"If you must go south, try Alaska," said Carl. *"You will be happier there, and in the spring, the colors are lovely."*

"No," replied Porter, *"I have decided. I am going to Hawaii."*

Porter found a large iceberg floating south. He packed a lunch and a toothbrush and climbed aboard.

He had floated only a short distance when he met Plimpton the Penguin. *"Porter, where on earth are you going?"* he asked.

"I am off to see the colors of Hawaii."

"Try Greenland," Plimpton suggested. *"It's much further east, but you will be happier there. And in the valleys, the colors are lovely."*

"No," replied Porter, *"I have decided. I am going to Hawaii."* And he continued drifting south.

A day or two later, Gertie the Gull landed on his iceberg to rest.

"*Porter, where on earth are you going?*" she asked.

"*I am off to see the colors of Hawaii.*"

"*Try Russia,*" Gertie advised. "*It is to the west, but you will be happier there. And the forest colors are splendid.*"

"*No,*" replied Porter, "*I have decided. I am going to Hawaii.*" And he continued to sail south. As he journeyed, Porter discovered that his iceberg was shrinking. As he neared Hawaii, it melted completely away.

Fortunately Weston the Whale swam up, and Porter climbed on his back. "*Porter, where on earth are you going?*" he asked.

"*I am off to see the colors of Hawaii,*" he said.

"*Don't be ridiculous, Porter. Stay on my back and I will take you back up to the North Pole,*" Weston said.

"*No,*" replied Porter, "*I have decided. I am going to Hawaii.*" And he climbed on an empty surfboard and rode it to the beach.

He walked down the beach. The sand burned his feet, the sun was terribly hot, and no matter how hard he tried, Porter could not take off his fur coat. He did not notice the beautiful colors, and he was not happy.

"*I have decided,*" Porter said, "*that I do not want to go to Hawaii after all.*"

IF YOU DO NOT CHANGE
DIRECTIONS, YOU WILL END
UP WHERE YOU ARE HEADED.

A SAD WILD WEASEL STARED INTO HIS EMPTY cooking pot.

He opened a great yellow book, the FOREST CREATURES GOURMET COOKBOOK. *"I'd love Plump Partridge Souffle for breakfast,"* he said, *"a Red Squirrel Ragout for lunch, and a Grey Mole Casserole for dinner."*

"But they're too fast for me," he sighed. Then he got a wonderfully wicked, weasely idea. He opened his cookbook and read, *"Pine Nut Pie: A delicious feast, especially tantalizing to partridges."*

He baked a tasty pie, took his finest tablecloth, and walked to Plump Partridge's roost. *"Plump Partridge,"* he called, *"I'm sorry for all those times I tried to eat you. I've baked a lovely pine nut pie. Won't you come down and let bygones be bygones?"*

"I won't come down, Wild Weasel, pine nut pie or not!"

"I'll sit far away. You can fly if I try to catch you."

"Maybe just one piece," Plump Partridge said.

She ate one piece and then another until she had eaten it all. *"That was really delicious, Wild Weasel. I'm just stuffed."*

"Good!" said Wild Weasel as he pulled out his bag.

Plump Partridge tried to fly back to her roost, but she had eaten too much.

"*Serves her right,*" Wild Weasel said, "*for eating so much.*" Then he took Plump Partridge home in his bag.

At lunch, Wild Weasel opened his cookbook and read: "*Giant Acorn Kabobs: A delicate appetizer, especially irresistible to red squirrels.*"

He cooked a platterful, took his finest tablecloth, and walked to Red Squirrel's tree.

"*Red Squirrel,*" he called, "*I'm sorry for all those times I tried to eat you. I've cooked up a lovely platter of giant acorn kabobs. Please come down and let bygones be bygones.*"

"*I won't come down,*" he said, "*crunchy kabobs or not!*"

"*I'll sit far away. You can climb your tree if I try to catch you.*"

"*Maybe just one,*" Red Squirrel said.

He ate one and then another until he had eaten them all.

"*That was really delicious, Wild Weasel. I'm just stuffed.*"

"*Good,*" said Wild Weasel as he pulled out his bag.

Red Squirrel tried to climb up his tree, but he had eaten too much.

"*Serves him right,*" Wild Weasel said, "*for eating so much.*"

At dinner, Wild Weasel opened his cookbook and read: *"Trumpet Mushrooms Teriyaki: A gourmet's delight, most appropriate when entertaining grey moles."*

He cooked a panful of marinated mushrooms, took his finest tablecloth, and walked to Grey Mole's hole.

"Grey Mole," he called. *"I'm sorry for all those times I tried to eat you. I've whipped up a lovely dish of mushrooms teriyaki. Please come up and let bygones be bygones."*

"I won't come up, Wild Weasel, marinated mushrooms or not."

"I'll sit far away. You can crawl down your hole if I try to catch you."

"Maybe just one," said Grey Mole. He ate one and then another until he had eaten them all.

"That was really delicious, Wild Weasel. I'm just stuffed."

"Good!" said Wild Weasel and pulled out his bag. Grey Mole tried to squeeze back down his hole. But he had eaten too much.

"Serves him right," Wild Weasel said, *"for eating so much."*

After his dinner, Wild Weasel patted his stomach. *"What I need now,"* he said, *"is a long nap in my hammock."*

He had just lain down when he heard somebody coming. It was Griff Grizzly.

"I hear you have a cookbook," he said, *"and have been trying out recipes. I've come to look up one of my own favorites."*

"You have?" Wild Weasel asked nervously.

"Ah, here it is," said Griff. *"I've been dying to try it."*

"What recipe is that?"

"It's Whipped Wild Weasel. All I need is a fat weasel stuffed with partridge, squirrel, and mole," he said and pulled out his bag.

Wild Weasel tried to run away, but he had eaten too much.

"Serves him right," Griff Grizzly said, *"for eating so much."* And soon Wild Weasel was stewing in his own pot.

> THOSE WHO SET TRAPS
> FOR OTHERS OFTEN CATCH
> THEMSELVES.

IN A TALL TREE ON A LONG branch lived a happy family of larks. Larry and Lucinda Lark and their children had a safe cozy home, plenty of food, and they had each other.

One morning as they ate breakfast, they felt their branch quiver. Looking up, they noticed a family building a new nest.

"I'm happy to see we're getting neighbors," said Larry.

Several days passed, and the lovely new nest was almost done. That evening the Lark family sat a bit more quietly as the sun shone softly on the new neighbor's nest.

"It's bigger, isn't it?" asked Lucinda.

"Yes, it is," replied her husband.

The next morning Larry arose before the sun and began to add to his nest.

Days passed and Larry and Lucinda noticed their neighbors were importing grass from the southern fields.

"I wish we had grass in our nest" said their oldest boy. "Our home must be colder and less comfortable than theirs."

So Larry spent many hours flying to the southern fields. Finally the Larks had a bigger, softer, warmer nest.

"Do you realize what a nice view of the river they have from up there?" asked Larry.

"You're absolutely right," said Lucinda. *"All I can see from here are the leaves."*

So Larry and Lucinda began working night and day, tearing branches from the tree. After weeks of work, Larry and Lucinda stood at the west window and admired their view of the river while their children played in one of the new rooms at the rear of the nest.

Just then a light breeze shook the branch. The heavy nest with all the unhappy Larks in it flopped over and landed on the cold, hard ground.

SOMETIMES LESS IS MORE.

ONCE THERE WAS A YOUNG goose named Grizelda who lived with a gaggle of geese behind a great high fence in a meadow filled with many good things to eat.

Each day Grizelda and her friends lunched on green grass and grubs. Every afternoon they walked along the fence line and yearned to sample the grass growing on the other side. All they could do was look with longing at the sumptuous banquet that was denied them by the fence.

The oldest goose was a grizzled old gander called Gordon. He'd been behind the fence longer than anyone. *"Why do we have to be confined behind the great high fence?"* Grizelda asked him.

"Confined? Is that what you think the fence is for? You silly goose," he said as he waddled away.

His answer puzzled her, so Grizelda went to see the wisest goose in the gaggle, a garrulous old girl named Gertrude. *"Why do we have to be confined behind the great high fence?"* Grizelda asked her.

"*There are so many good things on the other side.*"

"*Good things? Is that what you think is on the other side of the fence? You silly goose,*" Gertrude said as she waddled away.

Still bewildered, Grizelda went to speak with her best friend, a giddy young goose named Gretchen. "*Why do we have to be confined behind the great high fence? There are so many good things on the other side.*"

"*Why, Grizelda,*" Gretchen giggled,

"*we are not confined behind the great high fence. We have wings! We can fly!*" And with that, they spread their wings and sailed over the great high fence.

They landed at the edge of the forest and were so delighted by the grass and grubs, they never noticed the bright eyes of the lurking foxes grinning greedily in the trees beyond.

> FENCES THAT KEEP YOU IN
> MAY HAVE BEEN BUILT
> TO KEEP THINGS OUT.

SYLVESTER THE BULL wasn't afraid of anything. He butted trees and other bulls until his horns were broken and scarred. He didn't care. He was the strongest and most daring bull in the territory. Nobody could rope him or brand him, and that was how things continued for many years.

One day while leading his herd over a ridge, Sylvester came across an abandoned shack. It tipped forward where the cellar had caved in.

"That's the strangest looking shack I've ever seen," he said. *"I think I'll go have a closer look. Who's coming with me?"*

"Not me!" cried one.

"Nor I!" said another.

"It looks dangerous," said a third. *"And there is a 'KEEP OUT' sign on the door."*

"So much the better," Sylvester said as he swaggered down the hill. He circled the shack one way, turned, and circled it the other way. *"Not much of a shack after all,"* he said. *"Still, I wonder what's inside."*

He tried to peek in the window, but it was too high. So he strutted to the door and nudged it with his head. The door swung open, but before he could look inside, the door swung shut.

He butted the door again. It swung open and then it swung shut.

"I wonder what's making that door shut?" he said. Then he butted it again. The door swung open and the door swung shut.

"That's very unusual," he said. Then he butted it harder. The door swung open and the door swung shut.

Now he was more curious than ever. He butted the door again. The door swung open. But before it could shut, Sylvester pushed his head into the opening and let the door rest against his massive shoulders

"Now I can get a look inside," he said. He turned his head back and forth.

"Not very impressive," he decided. *"Nothing but old bottles, rags, and tin cans."*

But he could not see behind the door, so he went in a little further. In the corner was a pair of pants hanging on a nail. But he still could not see into the darkness behind the door, and so he pushed himself all the way in. The door swung open as he entered, but while he was turning around, the door swung shut. He was trapped!

Oh, how he fought. You could hear him up and down the valley. He thrashed his head

against the walls, but they were much stronger than they looked. He butted the door, but it would not give. He tried to jump through the window, but it was too small. He was in trouble, for he had no food, he had no water, and he could not get out.

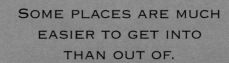

SOME PLACES ARE MUCH EASIER TO GET INTO THAN OUT OF.

ONCE THERE WAS AN ANTEATER named Arnold. He was quite fond of many parts of his body, but his favorite part was his tongue. He loved to talk. The only time he ever stopped talking was to use his tongue to find something to eat. He preferred ants more than anything else. He would extend his long sticky tongue into any likely hole, hoping for a tasty treat.

When he was not eating, he would talk to anyone about anything at any time. He was always certain that he knew

more about any subject than any other animal. And whether or not he knew more, the animals were all agreed that he could talk more about any subject.

Wherever you found someone willing to listen, you were sure to find Arnold.

Because Arnold needed a listener, his favorite companion was a friendly rabbit named Rodney. Rodney liked his ears as much as Arnold liked his tongue. Rodney could sit for hours and listen to the different sounds of the world around him. He loved to hear the wind blowing through the grass, the sound of the birds' wings as they flew overhead, and the scampering of mice dashing through their underground tunnels.

Rodney was not particularly fond of listening to Arnold's endless talking because he knew Arnold was not really an expert on everything,

but Rodney was too polite to say so. Anyway, he would rather listen than argue. So he listened while Arnold talked, and they were both happy. One afternoon as they strolled together, Arnold was explaining the flight patterns of migratory birds when he spied a tiny, dark opening in the ground. *"Look, Rodney,"* he cried. *"An ant hole. I can tell by the shape of the hole that this one contains an especially delicious and rare variety of tiny black ants."*

As Arnold extended his tongue, Rodney's ears were busy in the silence, listening at the tiny hole.

"Arnold," he said, *"I am not certain that this hole leads to a colony of ants. I hear a distinct buzzing under the ground."*

EeeeeOWW!

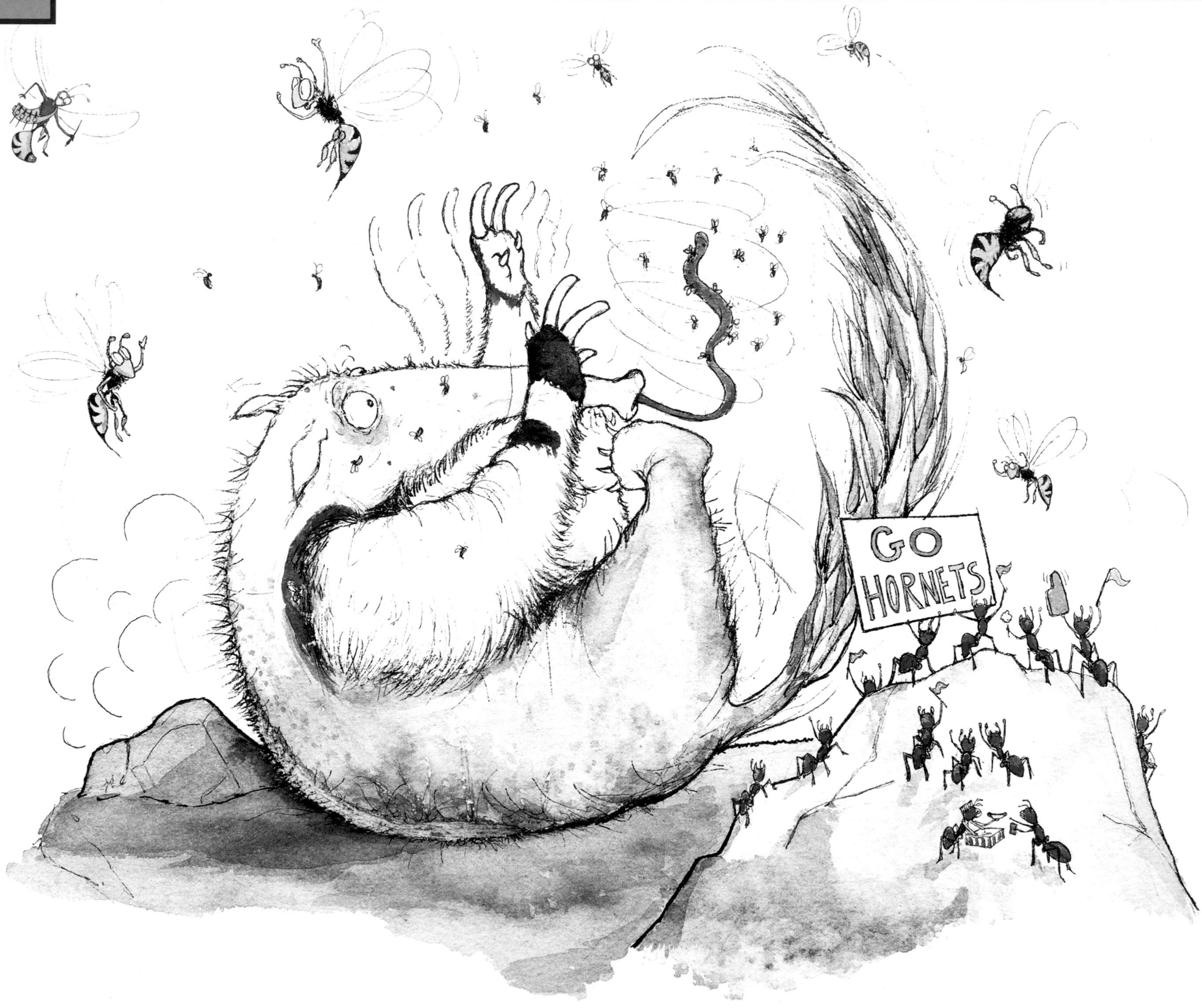
GO
HORNETS

"*Nonsense,*" responded Arnold. "*I know everything about ants!*" And he stuck his long tongue deep into the hole, his eyes shining with anticipation.

"*EeeeeOWW!*" cried Arnold as he jerked his tongue out of the hole. It was covered with angry, stinging yellow hornets. His tongue was swollen so bad that he could not speak or eat for four days. During this time he quietly sat by Rodney, listening to the sounds of the wind, the birds, and the mice.

YOUR EARS WILL ALWAYS
GET YOU INTO LESS TROUBLE
THAN YOUR MOUTH.

About the Authors

S. **MICHAEL WILCOX** recently retired as an institute instructor. A frequent speaker at Brigham Young University Education Week, Michael also conducts tours of historical Church sites all over the world. He received a bachelor's degree from Brigham Young University, a master's from Arizona State University, and a PhD from the University of Colorado. He is the author of many books and talks, including *House of Glory* and *What the Scriptures Teach Us about Raising a Child.* Michael and his wife, Laura, are the parents of five children and live in Draper, Utah.

TED L. GIBBONS and his wife, Lydia, are the parents of twelve children. He has been a teacher in the Church Educational System for almost four decades and currently teaches at the institute adjacent to Utah Valley University. He has published numerous articles, some poetry, and several volumes of fiction and non-fiction, as well as lyrics for several musical pieces, including some presented by the Mormon Tabernacle Choir. He is also an experienced stage performer and photographer.

About the Illustrator

MARK MCCUNE graduated from the University of Utah with a bachelor's degree in political science. While in school, Mark enjoyed working at the *Daily Utah Chronicle* as staff cartoonist. Mark has been an animation layout artist as well as an editorial cartoonist for several newspapers, including the *Deseret News.* He works full time as an auto, property, and general liability claim supervisor. Mark resides in Draper, Utah, with his wife, Elizabeth, and their two children.